Dear Parents:

Congratulations! Your child is taking the first steps on an exciting journey. The destination? Independent reading!

STEP INTO READING® will help your child get there. The program offers five steps to reading success. Each step includes fun stories and colorful art or photographs. In addition to original fiction and books with favorite characters, there are Step into Reading Non-Fiction Readers, Phonics Readers and Boxed Sets, Sticker Readers, and Comic Readers—a complete literacy program with something to interest every child.

Learning to Read, Step by Step!

Ready to Read Preschool–Kindergarten
• big type and easy words • rhyme and rhythm • picture clues
For children who know the alphabet and are eager to begin reading.

Reading with Help Preschool–Grade 1
• basic vocabulary • short sentences • simple stories
For children who recognize familiar words and sound out new words with help.

Reading on Your Own Grades 1–3
• engaging characters • easy-to-follow plots • popular topics
For children who are ready to read on their own.

Reading Paragraphs Grades 2–3
• challenging vocabulary • short paragraphs • exciting stories
For newly independent readers who read simple sentences with confidence.

Ready for Chapters Grades 2–4
• chapters • longer paragraphs • full-color art
For children who want to take the plunge into chapter books but still like colorful pictures.

STEP INTO READING® is designed to give every child a successful reading experience. The grade levels are only guides; children will progress through the steps at their own speed, developing confidence in their reading.

Remember, a lifetime love of reading starts with a single step!

Step into Reading, Random House, and the Random House colophon are registered trademarks of Penguin Random House LLC.

Visit us on the Web!
StepIntoReading.com
rhcbooks.com

Educators and librarians, for a variety of teaching tools, visit us at RHTeachersLibrarians.com

ISBN 978-0-7364-4267-1 (trade) — ISBN 978-0-7364-9012-2 (lib. bdg.)
ISBN 978-0-7364-4268-8 (ebook)

Printed in the United States of America

10 9 8 7 6 5 4 3 2 1

Random House Children's Books supports the First Amendment and celebrates the right to read.

FRIENDS ARE THE BEST!

adapted by Natasha Bouchard

illustrated by the Disney Storybook Art Team

Random House 🏠 New York

Meilin Lee is
thirteen years old.

She can always count on
her best friends.

Miriam is funny.
She is also clever,
and loyal to her friends.

Abby is spunky.

She is full of energy—

and tough!

Priya is quiet.

But she is always ready

to help her friends.

These four best friends love to sing and dance together.

Three of them like to
admire the cute store clerk.
Mei isn't so sure.

But they all love
the band 4*Town.
They want to go to
4*Town's concert!

Then one night,
everything changes
for Mei.

Ancient magic turns Mei into a giant, fluffy red panda!

Mei is upset.

Miriam, Priya, and Abby
cheer her up.

They sing and dance.
Mei's best friends
love her no matter what.

Mei calms down.
She turns back
into a girl!

Staying calm keeps
the red panda away.
Mei thanks her friends.

They have an idea.
They will use the red panda
to earn money to get
4*Town concert tickets.

Everyone loves
the red panda!
Mei takes photos
with her classmates.

Mei and her friends
also make red panda
items to sell.

The friends have
fun together.
They make a good team.

After a lot of hard work, they have enough money for the tickets. They celebrate!

Friends are the best.
Mei, Miriam, Abby,
and Priya always
have each other!